THE SECRET OF THE OLD WILLOW TREE

And Other Stories

By

Chrissie Ship

Shield Crest

ISBN: 978-1-912505-94-4

A CIP catalogue record for this book
is available from the British Library

MMXX

Published by
ShieldCrest Publishing Ltd
86 Springhill Road
Aylesbury, Buckinghamshire, HP18 0TF
England.
www.shieldcrest.co.uk
Tel: +44 (0)333 8000 890

For our Grandchildren; Rebecca, Claire, Luke, Jake, Olivia and Max because I want you to always have a little magic in your lives. Love you loads.

Nannie Chris

About the Author

Chrissie was born in Birmingham and now lives on the Suffolk Coast with her husband Ashley.

For many years she was a Diabetes Specialist Sister and upon retiring became a presenter on a local radio station.

She has always enjoyed writing short stories and poetry but this is her first attempt at having a story published.

One day whilst I was walking, walking all alone,
I met a little fairy sitting on a stone.
I asked her where she came from and where she went to bed,
Not a word was spoken, she only shook her head.
And when I went to touch her, to touch her tiny hand,
she spread her little fairy wings and flew to Fairyland.

MAGIC STORIES IN THIS BOOK

THE SECRET OF THE OLD WILLOW TREE

THE FAIRY PARTY AT THE BIG, BIG WILLOW TREE

THE STORY OF THE LITTLE FAIRY WHO GOT LOST

THE STORY OF THE OLD MAN IN THE LIGHTHOUSE

THE SECRET OF THE OLD WILLOW TREE

Once upon a time, deep in the forest, there was a big, big willow tree. It was so tall that you couldn't really see the top of it.

Olivia and Max used to go for a walk in the forest with their family, and one day, whilst they were walking past the big, big willow tree, Olivia and Max noticed there was something very different about the tree.

'Look Max,' said Olivia, 'there is a little door leading into the tree, I've never noticed that before.'

'No,' said Max, 'I've never seen it before either.'

They asked Mummy and Daddy what it was, and Mummy said she thought it might be a door leading into a fairy house.

Olivia and Max had never seen a fairy house before and wondered how it had got there. Daddy said he thought the very wise, old fairy had probably decided that the very big, big willow tree would be just the place for the fairies to live.

Hanging just above the door on one of the branches were lots and lots of sparkly bracelets and earrings which the fairies had put there for the children to see.

The very wise, old fairy, who was in charge of all the fairies in the whole world, had some very important news for the children.

He wanted them to know that the fairies had some very special magic fairy dust, which the fairies sprinkled around at night when all the children were fast asleep in bed. This fairy dust helped to keep everyone safe, but the most important thing was that it would only work if everyone remembered to stay two metres apart from other people when they were outside, and remembered to wash their hands properly for twenty seconds—as long as it takes to sing 'Happy Birthday' twice.

All the children everywhere decided they would do as the very wise old fairy said, and this, along with the magic fairy dust, would help to keep everyone safe.

One day, children will be able to see their grandparents, aunties and uncles, cousins and friends again. They will be able to play together and go back to school, but until then we are glad to see the fairy houses and to know that the fairies are helping us to stay safe.

THE FAIRY PARTY AT THE BIG, BIG WILLOW TREE

It was the Fairy Queen's birthday and deep in the forest next to the big, big willow tree, fairies from far and wide had come along to join in the celebrations.

There was special fairy cake and magic lemonade and all the fairies were having a wonderful time.

Suddenly one of the fairies, who had eaten lots and lots of special fairy cake and was feeling very full, asked why the tooth fairy wasn't there.

'Well,' said the Fairy Queen, 'the tooth fairy has to visit all the children tonight who have a tooth under their pillow, and she has to sleep today so that she will have lots of energy to fly around tonight.'

The other fairies wanted to know all about the tooth fairy. So the Fairy Queen explained that the tooth fairy looked through the window and made sure that the children were fast asleep and then she flew in the bedroom, left some money under the pillow, took the tooth and then flew away again.

Sometimes, if there were a lot of children to visit, it wasn't always possible for the tooth fairy to visit every child, but usually she managed to go back the next night.

The fairies thought that to be a tooth fairy must be lovely because you made all the little children happy, but it was a shame she had missed the Fairy Queen's birthday party.

'I know what we'll do,' said the fairy who had eaten lots and lots of the special fairy cake and was still feeling very full, 'we'll save some of the magic lemonade and the special fairy cake and the tooth fairy can have them when she wakes up.'

All the other fairies thought this was a very good idea, so they cut a big piece of special fairy cake and poured some magic lemonade into a special fairy cup and put them safely away, so that the fairy who had eaten lots and lots of special fairy cake wouldn't be tempted to eat even more!

When the fairies had finished their party, they tidied up and put all their rubbish away and the fairies who had come a long way had to fly home.

They had all had such a lovely time and when the tooth fairy woke up, she was very happy to see the special fairy cake and magic lemonade that had been left for her.

'Thank you so much,' she said, 'you are all very kind to have remembered me.'

The next day, Olivia and Max asked Mummy and Daddy if they could go for a walk deep into the forest and see the big, big willow tree with the fairy door. It was such a nice day that Mummy and Daddy said that they could.

When they got to the big, big willow tree, Olivia shouted to Max, 'Look Max, I can see some crumbs on the ground, right by the fairy door.'

Max had a look and said, 'Yes, so can I.'

Both the children got very excited and said they thought the fairies must have been having a picnic.

'Maybe,' said Mummy, 'they might have been having a party, because just like children, fairies have birthdays too.'

Daddy thought it might have been a birthday party, because just a little way away from the big, big willow tree he saw a little fairy candle that must have fallen off the special fairy cake.

Olivia and Max sat on a big log just by the big, big willow tree and watched to see if the fairies might come out of the little fairy door, but really they knew that fairies never show themselves to children; that's because they are magic and if they did, then their magic powers would go.

Everyone was really happy that they had been deep into the forest that day and wondered which fairy had had a birthday.

They decided that they would always walk to see the big, big willow tree deep in the forest and even though they knew they would never see a fairy, Olivia and Max said they would always keep looking, just in case.

THE STORY OF THE LITTLE FAIRY WHO GOT LOST

Once upon a time, deep in the forest, in the big, big willow tree, lived a little fairy called Isabella.

Isabella lived with her Mummy and Daddy and her fairy brothers and sisters and when she wasn't at school learning lots of fairy magic, she would play in the garden deep in the forest.

Isabella always wanted to know what else was deep in the forest besides the big, big willow tree, the fairy house and the garden, so one day, when no one was looking, she decided to go and find out for herself.

Because Isabella was only tiny, she couldn't quite reach

the handle on the door of the fairy house, so she pulled a chair over, stood on it and then she could just about reach up and open the fairy door.

Nobody saw her because her brothers and sisters were doing their fairy homework and Mummy was busy making some special magic fairy wings so that more fairies would be able to fly.

Daddy was very busy too, he was counting all the teeth that the tooth fairy had collected from under the childrens' pillows.

So Isabella turned the handle on the fairy door in the fairy house, opened the door and quickly ran down the fairy path before anyone noticed she had gone.

She ran and ran until she was quite out of breath and couldn't run any more and so she sat down on a little toadstool that was by the side of the path.

Isabella looked around and could see lots of trees and pretty flowers and then suddenly she heard a noise. She wondered where the noise was coming from and then she saw a little gnome sitting all alone and crying.

'Oh dear, please don't cry,' said Isabella, 'what's the matter?'

'Well,' said the little gnome, 'I'm lost, and I live on my own because I don't have any family and I can't remember where I live.'

Isabella found a big leaf and gave it to the little gnome to dry his eyes.

'I'll help you, little gnome,' she said, 'but I am only little too, and I have come a long way from my fairy house in the big, big willow tree deep in the forest.'

Isabella sat on the toadstool and thought really hard about how she could help the little gnome. At last she said, 'I think, little gnome, that we must look for someone to help us both find our way home, because I'm afraid I might be lost as well now.'

At this news, the little gnome cheered up and said he felt a lot better because he didn't want to be lost on his own, but he didn't mind being lost with someone else, especially a fairy, who everybody knows can do magic things.

'Well, little gnome,' said Isabella, 'I still go to fairy school and I am still learning fairy magic, so we need to find a nice friendly squirrel or hedgehog who knows the deep forest very well and can show us how to get home.'

The little gnome clapped his hands and said that sounded like a splendid idea, and so Isabella and the little gnome held hands and wandered deeper into the deep forest.

Before too long, they came across a hedgehog who looked like he was having a little sleep, but as Isabella and the little gnome got closer to him, he opened one eye and said, 'Yes, can I help you?'

'Yes please, Mr. Hedgehog,' said Isabella, 'my friend the little gnome and I are lost and can't remember our way home.'

'Oh dear,' said Mr. Hedgehog, 'that will never do. I will take you to see Sammy Squirrel who lives in the deep forest and keeps a register of exactly where everyone lives. He will help you find your way home.'

That turned out to be a very good idea, because Sammy Squirrel did indeed know exactly where Isabella and the little gnome lived.

'I shall ask the deer who lives in the deep forest to let you both have a ride home on his back, because you must be very tired,' he said.

Sammy Squirrel thought they should all have a piece of special cake that had been made that very day by Mrs. Squirrel along with some secret-recipe lemonade, while he wrote a letter to Isabella's Mummy and Daddy to say she was safe and would be home shortly.

He gave the letter to one of the birds that lived in the deep forest and he flew away to deliver it.

After Isabella and the little gnome were both full of Mrs. Squirrel's special cake and had drunk lots of her secret-recipe lemonade, they were ready to be taken home by the deer who lived in the deep forest. They held on very tightly and the deer ran swiftly, so it wasn't too long before they reached the big, big willow tree deep in the forest.

Mummy and Daddy were very pleased to see Isabella, but they were a little bit cross that she had gone out on her own because they had been very worried about her.

Isabella explained about meeting the little gnome who had no family of his own. Mummy and Daddy thought that was a shame and wondered if the little gnome would like to live in the fairy house in the big, big willow tree deep in the forest with Isabella, Mummy, Daddy and Isabella's brothers and sisters.

The little gnome thought this to be an excellent idea and said that he would help look after the fairy house in the big, big willow tree by keeping it very clean and tidy.

Mummy thought this would be just the right thing for the little gnome to do and so the little gnome moved in, but first he and Isabella had to promise Mummy and Daddy that they would never again go off on their own.

When Isabella was tucked up in bed that night, she thought about her adventure and about meeting a new friend, the little gnome, and about how kind the hedgehog and Mr. and Mrs. Squirrel had been.

Animals who live deep in the forest like to be kind and look after each other and that is why it is nice for us to be kind to animals in return.

The very next time that Olivia and Max went for a walk deep in the forest with Mummy and Daddy, they saw a toadstool just outside the door of the fairy house in the big, big willow tree and just by the side of it was a very tiny shoe.

'That,' said Daddy, 'looks very much like a little gnome's shoe to me because it has a pointed toe.' Mummy had a good look and said that she, too, thought it was a little gnome's shoe. Olivia and Max got very excited and said that maybe a little gnome had come to live with the fairies in the fairy house and maybe one day, if they were very lucky, they would be able to see him.

Well, you never know, so we must just keep on looking and hoping.

THE STORY OF THE OLD MAN IN THE LIGHTHOUSE

In a big, big red-and-white lighthouse overlooking the sea, lived an old man with a long, white beard. He had lived in the lighthouse ever since he could remember, and he helped to keep all the ships safe at sea by shining a big light so that the sailors would know he was there and would know where it was safe to sail.

The lighthouse keeper knew that there were lots and lots of lighthouses, so that meant that lots and lots of other people needed to work in them to make sure that all the ships, wherever they were, would be safe.

Max and Olivia's Grandad worked in a lighthouse and one day he told them the story of the old man with a long, white beard who lived in a lighthouse overlooking the sea.

This is how it began.

It was a very calm night and the stars were twinkling high in the sky. The old man with the long, white beard who lived in the lighthouse had said goodnight to his cat, made himself a cup of hot chocolate and was about to go to bed. Then he thought he should have one last look out to sea to make sure everything was as it should be.

He reached for his telescope and couldn't believe what he could see. In the distance, far away, he thought he saw a pirate ship!

The old man with the long, white beard scratched his head and thought he must have been mistaken. But no, he looked again, and it was indeed a pirate ship because it had a big black flag with a skull and crossbones on it. It was sailing towards land but only very slowly because there was no wind to help it on its journey.

'I must think of how I am going to stop this,' he said to himself. He sat in his big rocking chair and whilst he stroked his cat, he thought and thought. What really needed to happen was a storm or some wind that would blow the pirate ship back to the pirate island, but the air was very still, and the sea was very calm.

Once before, a long, long time ago, the old man with the long, white beard had helped to save a fairy ship that was being tossed about on the rough sea and the Fairy Queen was very grateful and said if he ever needed the fairies to help him he must send a message with one of the seagulls that lived on the lighthouse.

The seagulls all knew where the Fairy Queen lived, so the old man with the long, white beard sent a message with the seagull to say there was a pirate ship heading towards land and could the fairies help to stop it?

Back came the reply with the seagull that one of the fairies, who had been on the fairy ship that had been saved, had thought of a very good idea.

She knew that there needed to be a lot of wind to blow the pirate ship back to the pirate island, so she thought that if hundreds and hundreds of fairies held hands as they flew over the pirate ship with the big black flag with the skull and crossbones, then they would create a breeze that would blow the pirate ship right back to the pirate island. So that's what the fairies did, whilst the stars in the sky twinkled more brightly than ever and the moon shone to help the fairies see more clearly. The fairies flapped their wings to cause a big breeze and this meant that the pirate ship got blown right back to where it had come from.

The captain of the pirate ship wasn't very happy, but it was a long time before he dared to venture away from his island again. He knew that the old man with the long, white beard and all the other people who lived and worked in the lighthouses would always make sure we are safe from the pirates and that the fairies would always help too.

Olivia and Max were very happy that the fairies had helped to save us from the pirates and were glad to hear that the old man with the long, white beard who lived in the lighthouse had a cat to keep him company.